ROBin
Johns

A KIBBUTZ ADVENTURE

Photographers :	JOEL LOTAN
	JOSEPH DRENGER
	JOSEPH SHRAGAI
	DAVID PERLMUTTER
Narrative :	O. HILEL
Editor :	JOEL LOTAN
English Version :	RAY AND SIMON WOLF

FREDERICK WARNE & CO LTD : *London*
FREDERICK WARNE & CO INC : *New York*

DEDICATED TO MY WIFE RUTH
AND TO MY CHILDREN
JORAM AND MICHAL

© FREDERICK WARNE & CO., LTD.
LONDON, ENGLAND, 1963

LIBRARY OF CONGRESS CATALOG CARD No. 63-19357

PRINTED IN GREAT BRITAIN BY
THE BROADWAY PRESS LTD., LEWISHAM, S.E.13

INTRODUCTION AND GLOSSARY

*N*OT *very many years ago there were hardly any trees in Israel. Now there are forests all over the country. The tree, being one of the main symbols of the changing of swamps and deserts into cultivated land, is beloved in Israel by young and old.*

In every kibbutz children have their own farm on which they work, when not attending lessons. Work on the land is part of their education.

All the children seen in the pictures of this book, are living in a kibbutz.

DRUZE: *Moslems, living in Israel, speaking Arabic, but not considering themselves racially Arabs. Druze have their villages, among other places, on the slopes of Mount Carmel. They live in friendship with the Jewish Israelis.*

FENUGREEK: *a leguminous plant allied to clover.*

KIBBUTZ: *a large farm in Israel, usually with several hundred members, a unique combination of agriculture with a successful attempt to find a new way of a voluntary communal life.*

SHALOM: *means peace; "shalom" is the greeting most often used in Israel and everywhere else where Hebrew is spoken.*

A KIBBUTZ ADVENTURE

ONCE upon a time there was a kibbutz — one of the many in Israel. In that kibbutz — as in any other kibbutz — there lived many children. And it all happened on a beautiful spring day. There are often beautiful spring days in Israel, but this was a particularly enchanting one; the flowers smiled, the birds sang and the sun was more radiant than ever.

All the children felt happy, but only one of them put this feeling into action. Little Ruthi, elated because of the flowers, the birds and the sunshine, skipped into the classroom. Nobody was there, for the lesson had not begun yet. So she took a piece of chalk and wrote on the blackboard — as neatly as possible — two words in Hebrew: **Hayom Tiyul,** which means in English, "Today Walk," or "Today we shall go for a walk," or "Let us at least hope that there will be a walk today . . ."

But what would Tirzah say, Tirzah, the class teacher?

Then a miracle happened. When Tirzah entered the classroom, do you know what she said? She said, "Good morning, children! Today we shall go for a walk to the forest." And she hadn't even glanced at the blackboard. Well, wasn't that a miracle?

At first the children could not believe their ears, but then they jumped up from their seats and danced about the room, singing:

"Today — for a *walk*.
Walk, walk, walk!
Today to the fo-*rest*!
Rest, rest, rest!"

Believe it or not, in less time than it takes to tell they had tumbled helter-skelter out of the classroom, and into the spring and the sunshine . . . .

There they go: Tirzah, the teacher, Oozi, Danny, Ruthi, Ilan, then another Oozi, another Danny, another Ruthi, another Ilan, and still more children — freckled boys and laughing girls, everyone light of heart and fleet of foot . . . .

And in front of them all — guess who? Who else but Rammi and his great
friend, Rudy, lovely woolly Rudy! As you can see, Rudy was not another boy or
girl, but Rammi's dog.

The trees were tall, the bees were humming and the scent of wild flowers made the children happier still.

And so they came to the forest. There they found many, very many trees, and ten times as many flowers among the trees. In no time at all the children were shoulder-deep in the flowers, until it was difficult to say which were the flowers and which were the children for the faces of both children and flowers were happy and carefree.

When they had picked as many as they could carry they all sat down. Then the teacher said: "Just think! Some children live in places where there are no flowers growing. Let us send them some of these that we have picked today. We shall paste the most colourful flowers on cards and send them to children who are not as lucky as you."

"Fine, fine! A good idea," they chorused. Little Naomi added: "I shall send them my drawings, too." Whereupon Oozi, not to be out-done, announced proudly:

"And I shall send them a tractor." When everyone had had his say Tirzah began to tell stories . . . .

. . . . Beautiful stories they were and the children hung on to Tirzah's words, all of them gazing at her intently. But Rudy, the little dog, would not listen to the wonderful stories. He was interested in something else — an unusual scent was tickling his nostrils.

Well, what was it? What was happening? Why was this scent so exciting? This had to be investigated. A task lay ahead for him. The problem must be solved . . . .

Rudy was excited. But after a while he was more than excited — he was just not there any more. He had run off, with Rammi after him.

Rammi caught up with Rudy at a group of sycamore trees . . . .

. . . . and what they saw there — the dog and the boy — made them both very sad. Sycamore trees, small and large, were lying on the ground, uprooted, wounded, dying. Who had done this? Who could be so brutal and so savage? Suddenly, the dog made off once more, barking angrily. Rammi could hear Rudy barking on the far side of some bushes. Then some strange thing, some odd shape, scurried quickly out of the thicket and disappeared into another hiding place. The dog's hair stood up, and Rammi, too, felt a little frightened.

Trembling and sad at heart, the boy and the dog looked at the damaged trees. But Rammi soon woke up from his sadness. "I must tell Tirzah about this. I must tell the children," he thought.

And he ran, and he ran, all the way back to them.

"They are damaging the forest! They are uprooting the trees," shouted Rammi.
"What ?"
"Who ?"
"Where ?"

"We saw lots and lots of uprooted sycamore trees. We also saw — no, we didn't see it, but Rudy barked at it . . . ."

"At it? What do you mean? What was it? Who was it?" asked Tirzah excitedly.

"I really don't know," said Rammi, "because it escaped."

"Let's go and see," said Tirzah. The children followed her quickly.

It was a terrible sight . . . .

The children shuddered, and fell silent. Then Oozi, the smallest of them all, burst out: "Wait till I catch him! Uprooting our trees!" "We shall break all his bones," added Zivyah. "We shall chop him up for hamburgers." "He is crazy, just crazy."

The children shouted loudly, but they were very unhappy.

While all this was going on, a wagon, loaded with fenugreek, was making its way home, with Yerukham driving the pair of horses, but at the same time blissfully asleep (Yerukham, not the horses). He was musing in his sleep: "How pleasant it is to have a nap on a spring morning, lying on top of a wagon . . ." But the sweet dream was rudely interrupted by the noise of loud voices, and once interrupted the dream was spoiled. Yerukham cried out: "Quiet, please! Quiet! Don't disturb me. I mean it! I mean it!"

But by now he was quite awake. "Who is it? What has happened?"

"They are pulling up our trees!" "Must be a madman!" "We shall break his bones!" "Heaven help him if we get him!" The children were talking and shouting together and poor Yerukham could not understand a word. At last Tirzah managed to get a word in, and she told Yerukham the whole story.

"Come on! Jump on to the wagon, all of you," said Yerukham. "We shall go back home and there we shall decide what to do." He helped the children on to the wagon, one by one.

Meanwhile Hayim, the shepherd, appeared, riding as usual on his donkey. "Very strange," thought Hayim, the shepherd. "Very strange indeed! What are those children doing here this morning, riding on top of Yerukham's wagon? Very strange indeed!"

And whom did they meet when they came to the farm? Who else but Meshulam the foreman! The children repeated their story, for they knew that Meshulam would find a solution to the problem. "So that's that," said Meshulam, the foreman. "First of all we shall have to find Ephraim, the forester. Let's see what he has to say . . . ."

Another miracle happened. At that very moment Ephraim appeared in his ancient jeep. The jeep stopped and Ephraim, wearing his official-looking hat and smiling through his black, drooping moustache, jumped down. "Ephraim, Ephraim," the children called out in chorus.

"What's the matter?" Ephraim asked.

It was not long before he saw with his own eyes what had happened. And when he saw a young tree, bruised and wounded, he murmured: "This monster has no pity for young or old."

And Rammi added bitterly, "A villain, he is a villain."

While they were still talking, Ephraim stooped and picked up a bristle, which looked like a black-and-white knitting needle. "It was a *porcupine* that damaged the trees," he said, "but we'll catch him and teach him a lesson."

"What? A porcupine?" asked Rammi. "Why a porcupine?"

"When a porcupine is hungry he eats sycamores," explained Ephraim, "but this one is going to pay for it. Let's get the jeep. And you, Rammi, come with me. We shall go to the Druze village. I have an old friend there; Mustapha Halil is his name. He is a famous porcupine hunter. He will get the rascal."

The journey was not a long one and soon the ancient, coughing jeep arrived at the Druze village. The inhabitants were saying to each other: "Look who is coming. Isn't that Havadjah Ephraim, the forester?" "True, very true — and has he come to visit our Mustapha Halil?" "Yes, yes, aren't Havadjah Ephraim and Mustapha Halil as fond of each other as twin brothers?"

And lo and behold! Who was it who appeared on the high balcony adorned with geraniums and roses, if not Mustapha Halil himself, grinning all over his face and with his arm stretched out in a big welcome. "May Allah bless you! Come in, come in, my friends," he said in his booming voice.

For three and a half hours Ephraim, the forester, and Rammi were sitting on cushions, drinking coffee from small cups and listening to the stories told by their Druze friend. They were very interesting stories and Mustapha Halil told them quietly and slowly and in beautiful, flowery language, as is the habit of a Druze.

They find time to do everything slowly, and Mustapha saw no reason to hurry. But then came the moment for him to ask, "Why did you come, my friends? What can I do for you?" So they told him about the injured trees and the wicked porcupine.

"Tomorrow morning we shall go hunting," said Mustapha, and they raised their cups of the best coffee in the world.

The morning came, and the three set out for the forest: Ephraim and Mustapha on their horses and Rammi on a small cart. On the cart there was a cage. There is no need to tell you that the cage was for the porcupine — even the donkey knew that!

But Rammi had some trouble with the donkey who — in the manner of donkeys — suddenly decided that he had gone far enough. However, though donkeys may be stubborn, Rammi, the great porcupine hunter, was even more determined . . . .

Everything was set for action against the enemy.

They were advancing through hills, amongst rocks and wild flowers.

Rammi and his donkey were both sweating and breathing heavily.

Then suddenly, on a dusty path they saw the footprints of an animal.

Rammi stooped and picked up a sharp, pointed bristle, and he shouted, "Porcupine! Porcupine!"

"That's it," said Mustapha Halil. "Here we shall find his hideout."

"The cave! The cave!" shouted Rammi, looking anxiously at the frightening, dark hole.

"Hush," said Mustapha Halil. "We must work quietly." And as he began his work, his two friends carried the cage to the entrance of the cave.

Mustapha lay down and crawling slowly, inched his way into the dark cave.

Rammi's heart was beating wildly, from an excitement never before experienced in his young life. Ephraim, the forester, was staring ahead of him and his face was very serious. Porcupine hunting is a very difficult, even a dangerous, job. "I do hope all will end well," Rammi prayed silently.

There was a noise inside the cave. Then Mustapha reappeared, his hands grasping the head of the porcupine in an iron grip. Ephraim opened the door of the cage. Whoops! The rascal was a prisoner at last.

The porcupine was raising his bristles in anger.

Mustapha — dead tired — was perspiring, but happy and proud. "That was a nasty customer. It wasn't easy," he said.

Ephraim thanked him, shaking his hand warmly, while Rammi looked with
admiration upon the heroic Druze.

Now the porcupine was given into Rammi's care, and that was only just, for it was he who had toiled with the donkey and cart.

The procession was received with cheers and all the usual signs of rejoicing. For wasn't that a real victory? Rudy, the dog, jumped on to the cart and sat on the cage, as if to say: "Look what a monster-porcupine we have hunted and caught for you — we, I and my Rammi."

And then Tirzah came.

The little ones in the nursery wanted to know: "What is going on? What are the big children doing?" Their teacher told them a porcupine had been caught. So all the little ones shouted: "We want the porcupine! We want the porcupine!"

The porcupine was the only one who did not feel like celebrating. That he was not in a happy mood was rather understandable under the circumstances. He pretended that he was not at all interested in the proceedings around him. "Why don't they put me in some quiet corner?" he mused. "I suppose it is too much to hope that they will bring me a juicy piece of wood to eat and water to drink every day."

The porcupine should not have worried: his supply of food and water was assured, as well as a comfortable place to live. More than that, from now on he would enjoy the pleasant company and neighbourliness of chickens, ducks and all the other farm birds. And so, with all the honours due to him (were any really due?) the porcupine was introduced into his new home, in that special part of the kibbutz which had been given to the children as their own farm.

When that was done, Tirzah, the teacher, called out: "Three cheers for our hunters and heroes." The children cheered and cheered.

It is well known that real heroes never stay too long on the spot when they are no longer needed, and so Ephraim and Mustapha jumped on their horses and held up their arms in a greeting of peace and blessing.

"*Shalom, shalom*! Peace be with you," shouted the happy children.